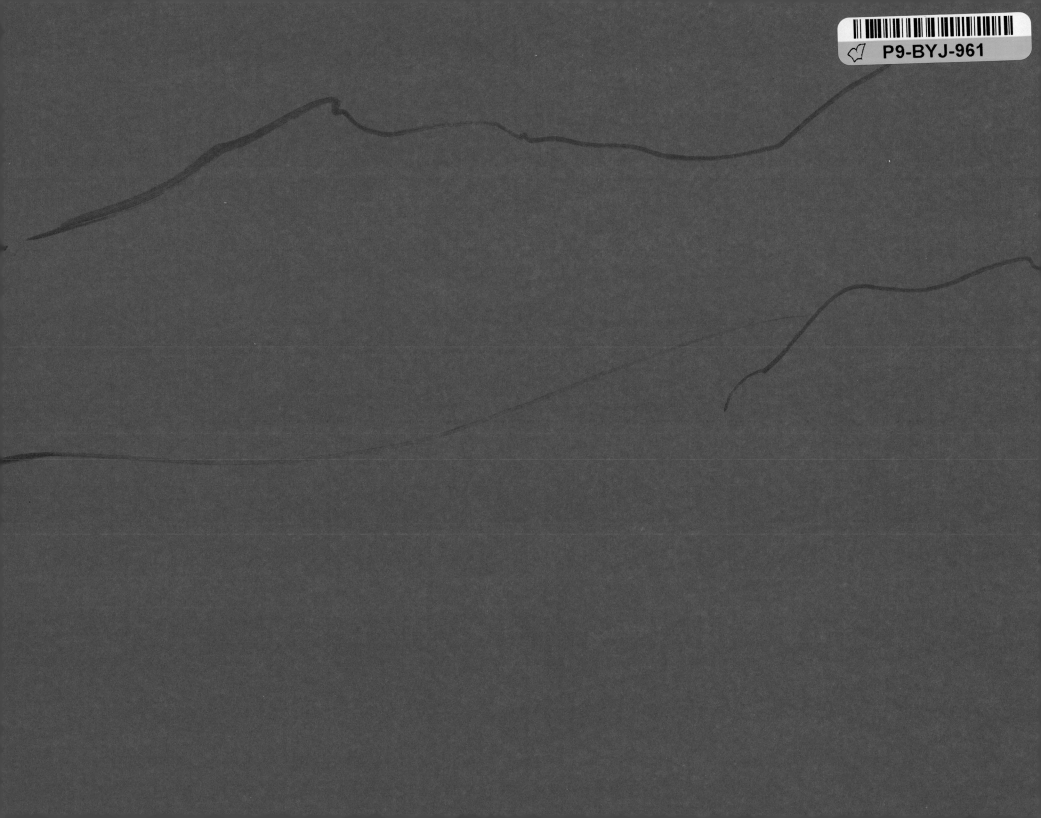
P9-BYJ-961

SEASIDE STROLL

SEASIDE STROLL

Charles Trevino · *Illustrated by Maribel Lechuga*

MAIN LIBRARY
Champaign Public Library
200 West Green Street
Champaign, Illinois 61820-5193

Charlesbridge

To YOU, you, and Anne—my supportive
spectacular spouse.—C. T.

To my parents and sister. Thanks for all
those summers on the beach.—M. L.

Text copyright © 2021 by Charles Trevino
Illustrations copyright © 2021 by Maribel Lechuga
All rights reserved, including the right of reproduction in
whole or in part in any form. Charlesbridge and colophon
are registered trademarks of Charlesbridge Publishing, Inc.

At the time of publication, all URLs printed in this book
were accurate and active. Charlesbridge, the author,
and the illustrator are not responsible for the content
or accessibility of any website.

Published by Charlesbridge
9 Galen Street, Watertown, MA 02472
(617) 926-0329 · www.charlesbridge.com

Illustrations done in Photoshop and Clip Studio Paint, with
 added watercolor textures made in traditional mediums
Display type set in Autumn Voyage by David Kerkhoff
Text type set in Colby by Jason Vandenberg
Color separations by Colourscan Print Co Pte Ltd, Singapore
Printed by 1010 Printing International Limited in Huizhou,
 Guangdong, China
Production supervision by Brian G. Walker
Designed by Jacqueline Noelle Cote

Library of Congress Cataloging-in-Publication Data
Names: Trevino, Charles, author. | Lechuga, Maribel, illustrator.
Title: Seaside stroll / by Charles Trevino; illustrations by
 Maribel Lechuga.
Description: Watertown, MA: Charlesbridge, 2021. | Summary:
 A child, a doll, and an adult go for a walk on the beach one late
 afternoon of a cold winter day, before heading home to dinner
 and a bedtime story.
Identifiers: LCCN 2019027503 (print) | LCCN 2019027504 (ebook) |
 ISBN 9781580899321 (hardcover) | ISBN 9781632897824 (ebook)
Subjects: LCSH: Dolls—Juvenile fiction. | Beaches—Juvenile
 fiction. | Parent and child—Juvenile fiction. | Picture books
 for children. | CYAC: Beaches—Fiction. | Winter—Fiction. |
 Dolls—Fiction. | LCGFT: Picture books.
Classification: LCC PZ7.1.T746 Se 2021 (print) |
 LCC PZ7.1.T746 (ebook) | DDC [E]—dc23
LC record available at https://lccn.loc.gov/2019027503
LC ebook record available at https://lccn.loc.gov/2019027504

Printed in China
(hc) 10 9 8 7 6 5 4 3 2 1

Scruffy shoes, socks, sweater . . . scratchy, silly scarf.

Step, step, sidestep . . . snow.

Slow steps—shuffle, straddle, saunter . . . sand.

Skip, spin, swing . . . seagulls.

Shells, stones, seaweed . . . surf.

Standstill.

Spectacular. Sparkling. Smile. Super!

Steady step, solid step, shaky step . . . stumble.

Swish . . . swirl . . . surge . . . surprised!

Slip . . . splash . . . sink . . . soaked!

Stretch . . . snatch . . . squeeze . . . saved!

Sopping shoes, socks, sweater . . .   salty, silly scarf.

Slide, slosh, squishy step . . . slush.

Sniffle, shiver, sneeze . . . shoulder.

Swift steps—scamper, scuttle, scurry . . . shower.

Spray, squirt, scrub . . . soapsuds.

Sweatshirt, slippers, supper . . . story.

Silence.

Safe. Snug. Sleep. Shh!

AUTHOR'S NOTE ABOUT THE WORDS IN THIS BOOK

Has a word ever clanked around in your head, demanding your attention, and then other words joined in? Each word brings its own ideas, impressions, and images. I began writing this story with the words *step*, *step*, and other words wanted to tag along, to go wherever we were headed. The story became similar to a poem. And it's a collection of sensory words (all starting with the letter *S*) about exploring a beach in wintertime. The story uses nouns, verbs, adjectives, and two interjections.

- **Nouns** are generally people, places, or things.
- **Verbs** are action words.
- **Adjectives** are descriptive words.
- **Interjections** are exclamations.

Did you notice the structure? The first eight lines and the last eight lines of the story match.

For example, the first line of the story goes like this:
Scruffy shoes, socks, sweater . . . scratchy, silly scarf.

That matches its partner line:
Sopping shoes, socks, sweater . . . salty, silly scarf.

And this is the eighth line of the story:
Spectacular. Sparkling. Smile. Super!

And it matches its partner:
Safe. Snug. Sleep. Shh!

The four lines in the middle of the story are made up of verbs with a few adjectives to increase the action.

The poem's rhythm and pace are meant to capture the wonder of exploration and discovery.

EXPLORING THE BEACH IN WINTER

Visiting a beach in the wintertime offers many sights and surprises. You might see:

- anemones, sea stars, crabs, and barnacles thriving in tide pools
- snow sculptures and sand sculptures standing side by side
- active birds
- certain stars and constellations from a different perspective
- various wintry cloud formations

What will you find?

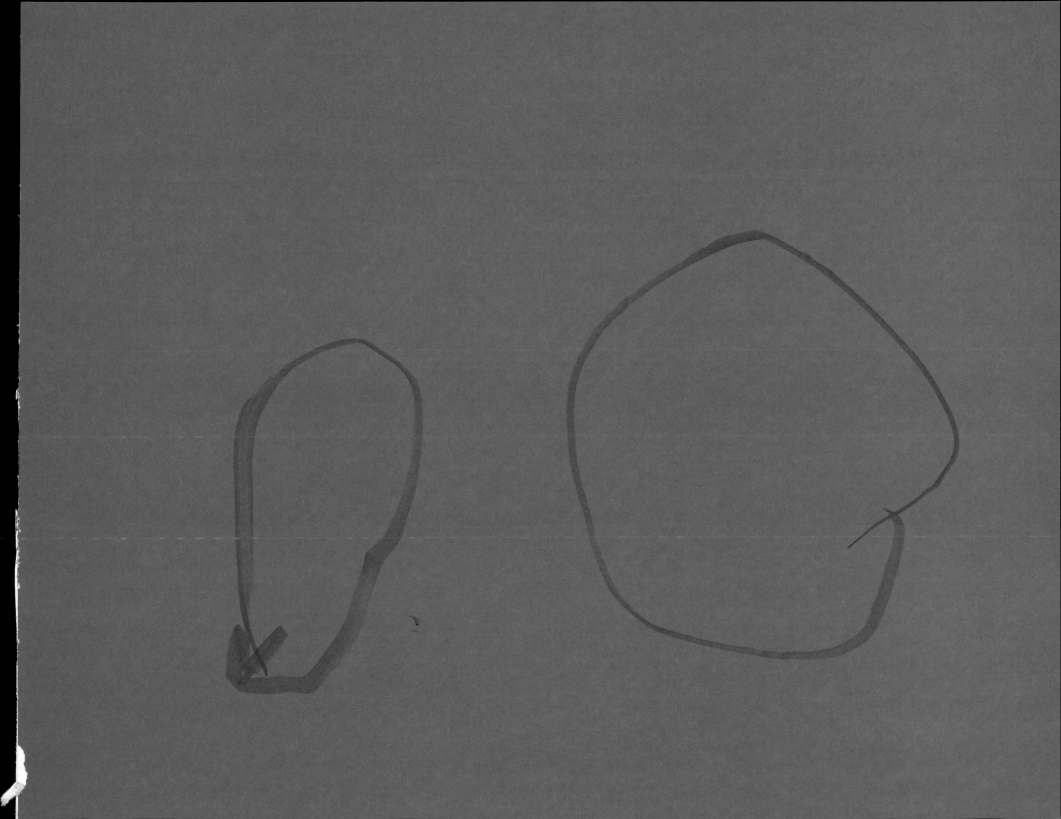

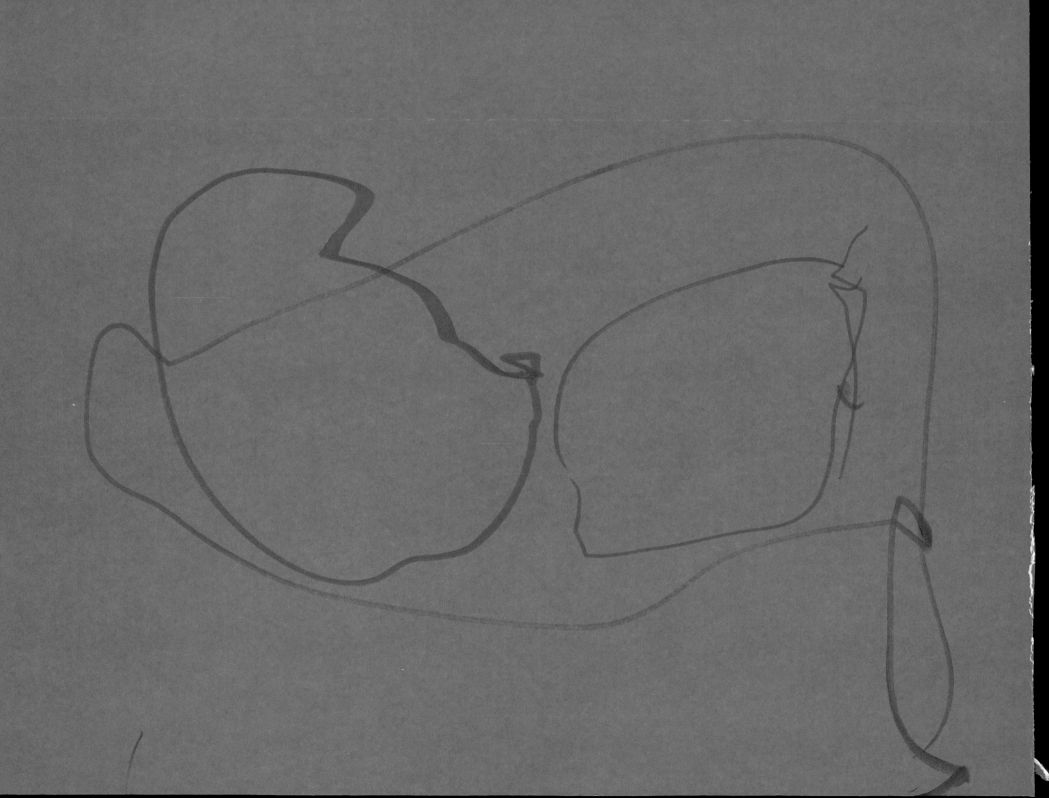